SHADES 2.0

KU-202-495

FOUR DEGREES MORE

Malcolm Rose

HIGH LIFE HIGHLAND	
3800 13 0055568 1	
Askews & Holts	Oct-2013
JF	£5.99

SHADES 2.0
Four Degrees More
by Malcolm Rose

Published by Ransom Publishing Ltd.
Radley House, 8 St. Cross Road, Winchester, Hampshire SO23 9HX, UK
www.ransom.co.uk

ISBN   978 178127 192 6
First published in 2008
This updated edition published by Ransom Publishing 2013

Copyright © 2013 Ransom Publishing Ltd.
Text copyright © 2013 Malcolm Rose
Cover photograph copyright © halbergman

A CIP catalogue record of this book is available from the British Library.

All rights reserved. No part of this publication may be reproduced, stored in a
retrieval system, or transmitted, in any form or by any means, electronic, mechanical,
photocopying, recording or otherwise, without the prior permission of the publishers.

The right of Malcolm Rose to be identified as the author of this Work has been
asserted by him in accordance with sections 77 and 78 of the Copyright, Design and
Patents Act 1988.

CONTENTS

ONE

East Anglia Reporter: Collapse of the house on the edge
BBC News: The real cost of global warming

My bedroom fell into the sea last year. I was watching on a safe part of the cliff, when the bit under my room gave way and ripped my house apart. A zigzag gash in the brickwork opened wider and wider. Wood splintered like breaking bones and my bedroom separated from the rest. Strips of wallpaper flapped around, plaster cracked into pieces, and the whole lot tumbled down the cliff. By the time it splashed into the North Sea, it looked like a smashed bird's nest. I remember my wardrobe door bobbing around on the waves, before I stomped away in a strop and kicked the four-by-four parked in the lay-by.

I wasn't the only one who saw my home break up. Someone filmed it on a mobile phone and sold the footage to the television people. It got played over and over again on the news. One moment, my room was perched on the edge of the cliff. The next, some of it was floating and the rest was sinking in an angry sea. I suppose that made my bedroom the most famous room in the country for a while.

I was thirteen at the time, and how did it make me feel? Never mind the sea being angry. It wasn't as angry as me. Angry is too small a word for how I felt. My brain boiled. I blamed the sea for being too rough. I blamed the wind and tide for turning each wave into a battering ram. I blamed the East Anglia cliffs for being too crumbly. But the telly news called it the real cost of global warming.

I did an environmental project at school. A few minutes on the internet told me that the TV got it right. It told me global warming was to blame for rising sea levels, stronger storms and coastal erosion. It also told me *who* to blame: oil and power companies, big business, the government, car drivers and air travellers, anybody with central heating and light bulbs and TVs and computers and every sort of plug-in electrical gadget. It was a very long list of anyone who uses energy. Really, it's people who are to blame for my bedroom taking that dive. But particularly, people in transport and power, who burn fuel and pump out carbon dioxide like there's no tomorrow. Made me glad I'd put a dent in that four-by-four.

It wasn't just a house that broke up. My family fell to pieces as well. I'm not blaming climate change for Dad walking out on us. That'd be silly. I guess it was the stress of living on the edge. By the time we had to move away from Happisburgh, Mum and Dad were at each other's throats all the time. Another gash had opened wider and wider.

Now, a year later, I live in Ipswich with

Mum and my old bedroom's not so famous. I still see it collapse sometimes, though. I can close my eyes and replay every detail, but that's not what I mean. Documentaries on global warming give it an airing now and again. Usually, it's a slow-motion replay – a slow slide into the sea. It's on the GreenWatch website as well.

I'm never mentioned. No one ever says, 'Poor Leyton Curry. There goes his bedroom.' No one ever says, 'I wonder what Leyton thinks about his personal space becoming a public display.' To them, it's just bricks, mortar and wood tumbling down. It's funny. Maybe scary as well. No one ever asked my permission to use my room as proof that the country's changing in a big way.

It's like when a goalkeeper makes a howler and the goal gets shown again and again. It gets lots of hits on YouTube and appears on a DVD of the most embarrassing things ever in football. That's my bedroom. Reduced to an *Oops!* moment on an environmental disaster DVD.

Still, there's nothing we can do about something as big as global warming, is there? We might as well just sit back and enjoy the sunshine – and the clip – one more time.

Wrong. I can do something.

TWO

ITV News: Terrorist threat causes Stansted chaos
East Anglia Reporter: The Cooler strikes again

I'm a one-person campaign. I can't walk past a four-by-four or a dirty great lorry without letting its tyres down. One in the back of the net for the environment. And it was me who did the graffiti at the airport, power plant and petrol station. I phoned a bomb threat to Stansted airport as well. 'Stop polluting the skies or the bomb goes off.' That worked a treat. The place went into meltdown for twenty-four hours.

When I was little, I always said I was going to be famous. Well, I was right. I'm headline news now. It's a bit much for the telly to call me a terrorist, though. I'm one of the good guys, trying to save the planet. That makes me the opposite of a terrorist. The local newspaper gets it right. They call me the Cooler. Get it? Someone who fights warming is a cooler. Not bad. And definitely not a terrorist.

I let rip about carbon dioxide and climate change at school, but no one knew I was the Cooler. I didn't let on until I couldn't keep it to myself any more. When I told my mate Keir, he looked at me with his mouth open.

'You? The Cooler?'

'Yes. Because of my bedroom. Because some whole islands are going to go underwater. They'll be wiped off the map.'

Keir shook his head.

'They're miles away. Nothing to do with us. Anyhow, I've said this before. You can't prove anything. Global warming might be down to cows farting and belching. And the sun getting hotter.'

'No chance,' I replied. 'It's us. I mean, adults. It's the way we live. Burning too much petrol and stuff.'

'But the Cooler's going a bit far. What does your mum say?'

'She doesn't know. But she'd be up for it. She went on all sorts of protests when she was young. Still does. Nuclear weapons, animal rights and stuff. She's always out marching for this and that. Tonight it's poverty, I think.'

'There's a bloke on a bike over there, watching you,' said Keir.

'What? Where?'

The man was on the other side of the road, outside the shops. Probably in his twenties. And, yes, he might've been looking at me. But he might not. Just in case, I gave him the finger and walked away.

Keir followed me, laughing.

'Even if you're right about the planet warming up, one boy with a spray-can doesn't add up to anything.'

'I know. But someone's got to take a lead and show the way. That's my job.' I flexed my muscles and puffed out my chest. 'The Cooler. But I'm not the only one really.

There's the GreenWatch people. They chained themselves to the gates of the oil refinery. And some of them were camped outside the power plant when I gave it a fresh coat of paint.'

'Big deal,' Keir muttered. 'The cops took them away.'

I looked behind me, but couldn't see the strange cyclist. 'I'm thinking of doing the oil refinery myself.'

'Doing? What do you mean?'

I tapped the side of my nose. 'That would be telling.'

Mum was out at one of her endless protest meetings. I changed into black clothes, waited until after midnight, and then sneaked out of the house. Grabbing the wire-cutters from the garage, I set out on the Cooler's next mission.

It couldn't be that difficult to avoid the oil refinery's security cameras and snip a way into the works through the wire fence. I knew what the place was like on the inside, because I'd seen it on telly. It was a tangle of pipes and tanks – like a climbing frame for giants. The oil in the pipes was controlled by those big valves with steering wheels on top. I reckoned I could screw the whole thing up if I closed a few taps that were open and opened a few that were closed. Simple.

Our housing estate was right at the edge of the massive oil refinery. Not a great view and not a nice smell for people like me, Keir and plenty more from school. Good cover for the Cooler, though. Peering round one house, I checked out the road. It was quiet and empty. But not dark. The factory's floodlights made the place look like a football stadium in winter. But I didn't want an audience for my little game. I'd be in deep trouble if someone spotted me. I carried on creeping through the estate.

I found what I wanted about half a mile further on. Thanks to a broken light bulb or whatever, one floodlight wasn't working. Below it, the wire fence was in the dark. It wasn't completely black, but that was okay because I had to see what I was doing. Hoping that any CCTV cameras wouldn't be able to make me out in the shadows, I dashed across the road and up the sloping verge. Kneeling by the fence, I grasped the wire-cutters in a sweaty right hand. I was about to snip the first diamond-shape when it struck me that the fence could be electrified.

No. Surely not. I'd never seen signs warning people to keep their dogs and babies away.

Squeezing the handle, the cutters made a satisfying click as the wire at the bottom snapped. And I wasn't electrocuted. Far from stopping my heart, my vandalism was making it pound like crazy. Great stuff.

Another few seconds and two more snips. I reckoned I'd have to clip away for a minute before I could make a gap big enough to crawl through. I was concentrating on what I was doing, but I was also listening for cars, voices or alarms going off. There was nothing.

I wasn't going to chop out a complete hole. That wouldn't have been clever. I just needed to cut enough to bend the wire back to make a door. Then, after I'd got through, I could fold it back into place. Anyone passing would've probably seen a hole but I doubted that they'd notice a slit.

When I thought I'd cut far enough up

from the ground, I started going across. Only a few more snips and I'd be able to bend the netting inwards. But I wasn't quick enough.

I don't know exactly what told me – maybe a footstep, or the sound of a breath – but I knew someone was behind me. Spinning round, I saw two men. They didn't look like security or police. No uniform.

The one on the right looked familiar. He whispered, 'That's not a good idea right now.'

'What?' I exclaimed.

'Keep your voice down. Come on. Come with us.'

'What?' I repeated, this time in a hush.

'Forget what you're about to do.'

'You've got to be – Who are you?'

'WHOOP.'

'What?' I said for the third time, getting

up off my knees and holding the wire-cutters out like a knife.

The man sighed impatiently. 'It stands for We Have Only One Planet. We're the people who run the GreenWatch website.'

'How did you know I was – '

Interrupting, he said, 'We were protesting at the power plant when you did your bit of graffiti. Ever since, we've been ... keeping an eye on you.'

'Following me!' Lowering my voice again, I muttered, 'You're the bloke on the bike.'

'My name's Robin.' He glanced up and down the road. 'It's time to go.'

'Are you going to bundle me into the back of a car?'

Robin smiled.

'We wouldn't be very green if we went around in cars kidnapping people, would we? We just want you to come and have a chat with Beth.'

'Beth?'

He nodded.

'We admire what you're doing here, but it's just a prank really.'

'How do you know what I'm going to do?'

'Look. We're planning something much bigger, and what you're doing will mess it up. There's a good time to use your hole in the fence, but it's not now. Come and talk to Beth.'

At last, the second man spoke.

'This way,' he said quietly, turning his back and making for downtown.

THREE

*The Mirror: Environment Minister reveals
green plans*
GreenWatch website: Four degrees more

It turned out that Bethany Morris-Steward
was WHOOP's chief activist. The green
queen. She looked like a university student.
Perhaps she was. Dressed in denim, she was

thin with tangled, brown hair and glasses. She spoke quickly and passionately about the environment, like she was in a rush. She reminded me of a clock that had been wound up too much. Her hands were whizzing round to get rid of all that stored-up energy.

Unable to keep still, Beth paced up and down.

'Some people see us as eco-bullies. That's rubbish. The power and transport industries are the bullies around here. They're the ones doing the damage. Cars and planes. Oil, coal and gas.'

'Yeah,' I said, because I thought I should say something.

She gazed at me for a few seconds and then nodded. 'You ought to join us. We need all the recruits we can get. On top of that, if you care – *really* care about the planet – you'll be able to do much more with WHOOP behind you. We're a big organisation now.' She barely hesitated. 'You know the Drax Power Station up north? Its chimney chucks out the same amount of carbon dioxide as a quarter of the traffic on the country's roads. It was on the news last week. That was our people who chained themselves to the conveyor belt. Two more climbed a cooling tower. High profile stuff. You can be in on that sort of action.'

'I'm no good with heights.'

Her sharp face formed a smile for the first time.

'I think we can find something nearer the ground for the Cooler. Once, we blocked the M11 with a sit-down protest across all six lanes.'

In a way, she reminded me of Mum. It would be good to belong to her family of rebels.

'What are you doing about the oil refinery?'

She flicked her hair behind her ears for the hundredth time.

'First, let me say it's not just about shouting the message in people's faces. It's not just about picketing electrical shops, car makers and airports. We're fighting quietly behind the scenes as well.' She picked up a newspaper from the table and pointed at the headline about the Government bringing in some eco-friendly policies. 'See? A Minister's suddenly cleaned up his act.'

'Has that got anything to do with you?'

Beth laughed.

'He hasn't really come over to our way of thinking. Politicians are moved by pressure, not principles. And this one's under pressure because we know a dirty secret about his private life. Something that would kill his career. We told him we'd splash it all over the internet unless he forced our agenda through parliament.'

'You mean, he's gone green because you're blackmailing him?'

She nodded.

'The heat he's feeling is nothing to do with global warming, but it's working, so … ' Beth shrugged. 'The end justifies the means.'

'I like it. Good trick.' Then I tried my luck again. 'And what about the oil refinery?'

'I could quote a lot of frightening facts. Just one will do. The oil that the planet used in the whole of 1950 would only last six weeks now. Half of it goes into transport.' She shook her head. 'Ridiculous. It's got to stop. If our minister under pressure doesn't deliver, we're going to show him how serious we are.'

'By doing what?'

Beth paused. 'Let's talk again in a few days, Leyton. Give everyone time to think. Then let's see how you feel about joining in. If we can build up a bit of trust, maybe – ' She grinned instead of finishing what she was saying.

I logged on to the GreenWatch website to see what all these frightening facts were. It made pretty grim reading. One page showed what's likely to happen if we let the planet's temperature go up by another four degrees. Four degrees doesn't sound like much, but it'd make a lot more bedrooms fall into the sea.

Southern Europe, the Amazon rainforest and western USA are deserts. A third of the world's land does not have enough fresh water to support human life. Forest fires are out of control. Summer temperatures in southern England are over 40°C. Heatstroke kills tens of thousands of people. Millions of people are starving. Tens of millions are forced to move into already overcrowded countries that still have water and food.

The West Antarctic and Greenland ice sheets are melting. Sea levels are metres higher and rising. Low-lying islands in the Pacific Ocean, like the Maldives, are drowned. Eventually, central London, Miami, Manhattan, Bangkok, Shanghai and Mumbai will be flooded. Half of the world's population will have to move to higher ground. Coastal erosion threatens 2 million people in the UK.

Extreme floods in Bangladesh, the west coast of India, Vietnam, Florida, and northern Egypt.

Mosquitoes have spread and threaten 80

million more people with malaria.

The strength of wind in destructive storms has increased by about 20 per cent. Super-hurricanes threaten the major cities of Hong Kong, Tokyo, Shanghai, Brisbane and New York.

In the long-term, four degrees more will melt all polar ice, and sea levels will rise over 50 metres. The UK would be a scattering of islands and Oxford would be on the coast.

Looking over my shoulder, Keir grunted.

'Laying it on thick, aren't they?'

'Even if it's only half right … '

'Come on. Anyone can say crazy things. In the next five years, Ipswich will win the Premiership.' He shook his head. 'Ain't going to happen.'

'But this is science.'

'It's a bunch of people spouting stuff to scare you.'

'It's working,' I replied. 'And you know what makes me angry? Grown-ups. When we do something wrong, they always say, "You made that mess, so you clear it up." Talk about two-faced! They're the ones who are messing the Earth up, so they should clear it up but, no, they won't. They won't even give up their four-by-fours. It's not fair. They're old. They're not going to live much more, but we will. It's our planet. And it's knackered. Thanks very much for handing over a clapped-out world.'

'So, what are you going to do about it?'

I didn't answer. But, like Beth said, it's got to stop. We do have only one planet. I've got to ram the point home by stopping the oil refinery. It's the right thing to do. The only thing to do.

FOUR

*The London Paper: Environment Minister in
shock resignation
The Sun: Green plans on backburner*

'Huh. The green spell didn't last long,' Beth
muttered when she saw the news. The
politician she was blackmailing had quit his
job, so her plans to force the Government

to fix the environment lay in ruins.

'You know what's happened, don't you?' Robin said angrily.

Beth nodded as she screwed up the newspaper and threw it aside.

'It's not hard to guess. I smell LOP in action.'

It's like they were talking in code.

'What do you mean?' I asked.

Beth wrapped her hair around her fingers.

'It's a fair bet the League of Oil Producers – a pressure group that denies global warming – knew the minister's grubby little secret as well. Like us, they've threatened to reveal all, I imagine.' Beth shook her head. 'If he tried to push green laws through, LOP would leak his private life to the press. If he didn't, we'd talk instead. He'd lose either way, so he's got out quick. Anyway,' she said, 'it means LOP is playing rough. So we've got to do the same. It's time to show everybody the damage the oil industry does. It's our duty to clean up a dirty industry.'

I'd skipped school. After all, saving the planet was more important than a few GCSEs. I was ready and willing for action. I said, 'Totally agree.'

The green queen nodded. 'You're like me. You let your anger show. You let it all out.'

'Better out than in, my mum always says.'

Beth smiled in a serious sort of way.

'Robin bottles it all up until it gets too much. Then he explodes. Anyway, if we're going to get our message across, we've got to hit the refinery hard. Maximum impact.'

At that moment, revenge for my bedroom and fixing the planet seemed very close.

'Good idea.'

Beth gazed at me for a few seconds, as if making her mind up about me, and then said, 'All right, Leyton. I think I know you well enough.'

She hardly knew me at all, but I was pleased that she was about to let me in on her plan of action.

'Here's what we do.' Her voice was almost a whisper. 'We're going to have a massive protest outside the oil refinery. I'll get all our people involved, so we'll make ourselves a really big nuisance.'

'And you want me to join in?' I asked.

Beth shook her head.

'No. We'll keep the police and security guards busy by storming the gates, but the real action will be happening quietly inside. *That's* where you come in.'

'Oh?'

'I bet it feels good,' she said, nudging my arm. 'You're the most important part of the whole thing.'

I should have asked, 'Why me?', but I was blinded by anger over my old bedroom and everything that went with it, so I said, 'Great!' It felt fantastic to be part of a group instead of a one-person campaign. A bit like having a proper family again.

'We'll just be the distraction. You'll do the sabotage. You'll be the green champion.'

'What do you want me to do?'

Going over to the table, she unfolded a large plan of the factory.

'See these three containers in the middle? They're the main storage tanks for the refined oil.' She stabbed her finger at them. 'That's what you attack. The heart of the business.'

'How do you mean?'

'If they went up in flames ... Think of a fantastic firework display and multiply it thousands and thousands of times. That's one impressive show.'

I stared at her, but couldn't speak.

'We've got a device,' she said. 'It'll only take a few minutes to show you how to set it up.'

'A device?'

'Yes.'

'You mean a bomb?'

'Just something that'll burst the tanks. Imagine it. The factory supplies a huge amount of oil and petrol. Knock it out and this country's ability to pump out carbon dioxide will take a massive hit. Utterly enormous. It'd take an age to recover.'

'But a bomb – ' I took a deep breath. 'Won't people get hurt?'

'At night, there's hardly anyone on site.'

She paused and looked into my face. 'Let me ask you this. What would you do if your best mate was locked in a room that was filling with water? Would you go and find the key and get him out straight away, or wait to see if it developed into an emergency and then fetch the key when it's too late?'

'No-brainer. I'd go straight away, but – ' She was talking in riddles again.

'We could wait for the climate to get out of hand and wish we'd done something before it was too late,' Beth said, 'or we could act now. We need you to do this, Leyton, because you're not known to the police. We are. We're watched. Is the Cooler with us?'

'All right. Count me in. But … I just don't want to hurt anyone.'

'It'll be okay. Trust me. You go and work with Robin on the device.'

The night was warm and sticky. Or was it just me? I had the device – as Beth and Robin called it – in a haversack. I was damp where it pressed heavily against my skin, and I could feel the sweat trickling down my back. But the night air was muggy anyway. I was feeling the effects of global warming, as well as carrying the bomb.

But it was all for a good cause. It wasn't as if I was a terrorist, suicide bomber or anything. I was only going to wreck some storage tanks, oil and a business. No people were in the firing line. It was the right thing to do.

Without a sound, I crouched down in that circle of darkness and folded back the wire. The hole in the fence reminded me of a dog kennel. I took my backpack off and carefully pushed it through first. Then I crawled into the oil refinery. Standing up in enemy territory, I strapped the bag on to my back again and looked around. So far, no problem. I pointed the tiny torch at my wrist and switched it on for a second. Nearly quarter past midnight. It wouldn't be long now. I just needed to wait a few minutes.

I'd memorised the map. I knew where I had to go. Across an access road and slightly to the right. There, I'd see a large overhead pipe and I could follow it to get to the centre of the factory. It would be like following an artery to the heart of a body.

My new friends were going to kick up a fuss near the main gates at twelve fifteen, but I didn't know exactly what would happen. The siren took me by surprise. I dived to the ground, hoping I hadn't been seen or set it off. It was very loud. Everyone on the housing estate would be waking up and cursing the factory for being so close.

The siren screamed into the stillness and I could see lights coming on. People in uniform were rushing around. They were a long way away and they weren't coming in my direction. Beth must have started the riot. Hopefully the WHOOP protesters had attracted the attention of every guard in the grounds. The siren was the starting pistol for my mission.

I got up again and ran, crouching a bit, towards the pipe. The device clunked against my back, reminding me it was there, reminding me how important I was to the group and to the Earth.

The place stank like a big, dirty machine. I turned left and went along under the pipeline. I was on a tarmac track between two low buildings. There were no lights on, so I couldn't see what happened inside. Coming up to a much bigger road, I slipped on an oily patch but managed to keep on my feet. I felt like a little kid, looking left and right and left again before crossing. But I wasn't looking for cars and lorries. There weren't any. I was looking for security guards or anything that might give me away. There were all sorts of strange pieces of equipment down one side, but I didn't see any danger so I dashed across the road.

I had to hope that, if I'd been caught on CCTV, no one was watching the pictures. I had to hope that everyone was dealing with the green queen and her rebels.

I jumped in shock when the siren stopped. The sudden silence surprised me. Someone must have turned it off, because it had done its job. It must have alerted all the security staff and maybe the police.

The track continued. There were three pipes above me now and one at ground level. There was also the constant hum of machinery – or perhaps it was the noise of oil churning through the pipelines.

I gasped when I saw a torchlight bobbing ahead of me. Before the beam came in my direction, I swerved off the track and flattened myself in the gap between two cabins. I could feel my blood pounding through my arteries, my own heart on the point of exploding. I held my breath.

It wasn't long before I could hear footsteps. Next, I saw the torchlight sweeping from one side of the pathway to the other, searching. Then came the guard in a dark-blue uniform. It was a woman, and I was lucky because she wasn't really paying attention. She had a phone pressed to one ear.

'Yes. I'm down H8, near Distillation Unit 4. No. There's nothing.' She listened to the reply and then said, 'Sounds like you need all the back-up you can get. Okay. I'm on my way.' She set off at a sprint.

I let out my breath and my heart rate slowed a little. I came out from my hiding place a minute later, hoping that the woman was the last guard to be called to Beth's noisy demonstration.

With long, empty buildings on both sides and large pipes above, the path reminded me of a cave or tunnel. There was a light at the end. In the distance, the track led to a monster floodlit roundabout. In the centre were the three storage tanks and they rose up into the night sky like tower blocks. I hurried towards my target.

Far away, there was the sound of shouting, banging and whistling. The activists were putting it all on for me. They were the defence and I was the striker up front. We all belonged to the same team. I was part of something big, and even if everything went wrong, I knew I wasn't alone. Lots of people were on my side.

By the time I reached the ring road around the tall containers, sweat was pouring down my back. A petrol tanker and several vans were parked in front of me, and beyond them were the towers of oil, soon to be the most powerful fireworks the country had ever seen. But right now, the place was quiet and still.

There was no way of hiding. I'd have to dash across, put the device at the base of one of the giant containers, set its timer, and hope that I wasn't spotted. When the first tank exploded, it would tear holes in the other two and the whole lot would go up in flames. I'd have ten minutes to get away. No problem.

Taking a deep breath, I sprinted for the gap between the petrol tanker and the works van parked behind it. A quick look around. A decision. I made for the closest storage tank. Kneeling beside it, I yanked my haversack off, ignoring the clammy shirt stuck horribly to my back.

This was it. This was what the Cooler did. Just as Robin had shown me, I turned the timer to the ten-minute mark. I didn't hang around. I just looked up once. The dull metallic tank was enormous, like a great big fat rocket, full of fuel waiting to be launched.

The clock was ticking. The countdown had begun.

FIVE

The Mirror: Oil refinery bombed
The Guardian: Death at green protest

Grinning to myself, I scrambled through the
hole in the wire fence. Straightening up, I
felt good. Really good. I'd done it! The
Cooler had completed his most daring
mission so far. With six minutes to spare.

Taking a deep breath, I made the call to Beth.

Even before she spoke, I could hear the background din of the protest. I didn't wait for her to say anything.

'It's me,' I almost shouted. 'The Cooler. Mission complete!'

'Brilliant. Well done. I'll move everyone out.'

I was more than surprised. There was a sudden sickly feeling in my stomach. 'What do you mean? Why? It's just going to be a big firework.'

'Very big. You've lit the blue touch paper. Now we all stand well back.'

I hesitated.

'What are you saying? Where's far enough back?' I was beginning to panic. 'What about the estate? Is that far enough away? Me and Keir live there.'

'It's too late, Leyton. You've done it. But just think how many lives you save down the line. A few casualties now, the planet saved for later. It's a good deal.'

'You conned me!'

'It's not like that, Leyton. Look, I'll send Robin down. He'll sort you out. But right now, I've got to pull everyone out.'

Stunned, I stood there with a dead phone in my hand. I was shivering, not with cold, but with horror at what I'd done. Beth's words had convinced me that the fireball would roast the whole area, including the housing estate. Not even the green cause was worth that sort of sacrifice. There'd be deaths. There could be hundreds, for all I knew. And there'd be horrible injuries.

The Cooler had turned into a terrorist, after all.

Belonging to the environmental group

had given me a warm glow, but the feel-good factor had now gone. I didn't want the same thing as the rest of the team any more. My strike against the oil refinery didn't feel right. I felt nervous and cheated. And alone.

I glanced at my watch by torchlight. Four and a half minutes to go. Was that enough time to undo what I'd done? I'd got out of the oil refinery in four minutes. I had to give it a try. I dropped the phone, ditched the backpack and threw myself to the ground. As fast as I could, I crawled back into the grounds of the factory. There was no time to hide and creep. I dashed back to the overhead pipe and ran along the path. The narrow way was more like a racetrack now.

I still felt important – more important than ever – but everything had changed in an instant. I had to save lives instead of the planet.

The noise of the protest at the main gates had faded, but all I could really hear were my own footsteps. And my heart hammering in my chest. Somewhere, a car engine revved up. I took no notice of it.

Panting, I arrived at the road that ringed the storage tanks. This time, there were two people in uniform standing a long way to my left. I realised that if I sprinted across the road, I'd look very suspicious. They would come after me. And if they stopped me, that would be the end of me, them, the whole factory and probably the estate. I glanced at my watch. Fifty-five seconds.

I didn't know what to do.

Another guard appeared. This one was coming from the direction of the main entrance. He was returning from the battlefront. And that told me what to do. Now that the protesters had gone, there were bound to be staff coming back. No one would be surprised to see workers wandering around the site. Maybe, if I looked confident … Maybe if I didn't look suspicious …

I drew myself up to look as tall as possible and strolled across the road. I tried not to hurry, tried not to draw attention to myself. I tried to keep calm but my pulse was racing. Once I'd slipped between the parked lorry and van without being challenged, I felt better. I wasn't so visible there. And the storage tank was in front of me.

Thirty-seven seconds. It was then that I realised. Robin had shown me how to set the timer. He'd never shown me how to stop it. I couldn't hold myself back any more. I darted to the nearest container and dropped to my knees. The dial on the top of the bomb was counting down the final twenty-five seconds. I grabbed hold of it and tried to stop it clicking round towards zero. Maybe my hand was slippery with sweat. I don't know. But it just kept going. I couldn't halt the countdown.

Turning the device over with trembling hands, there was nothing like an on/off switch. I'd set it going and there was no clear way to stop it.

I looked around in fear. A police officer had just pulled up and got out of her car. In her hurry, she'd left the door open. That was it. My only chance.

Thirteen seconds.

I grabbed the bomb and hurtled towards the car. Someone somewhere shouted, 'Oi! You!'

I threw the device inside the police car, slammed the door shut and didn't stop running.

I was a few metres down the track when it exploded. I thought my ears had burst. And the blast picked me off my feet and flung me forward. I guess I screamed. I can't remember. I rolled over and over, like a footballer fouled at full speed. But I wasn't pretending. Every muscle seemed to ache. I felt blood on my right cheek. But I got to my feet. I had to. I had to get away.

Behind me, the mangled wreck of the car was blazing and oil workers were running around and shouting madly. But the storage tanks were safe. The people were safe. The estate was safe.

Gasping for breath and swaying unsteadily, I raced back down the path towards my hole. In the total confusion of the explosion behind me, I was getting away. My head, chest and legs were throbbing horribly, but I'd done it. No one had got hurt – apart from me, and I was just grazed and bruised. And confused.

I came out from under the pipeline, lurched to the right and made for that doorway in the netting. I was so relieved, so desperate to get out, that I didn't notice the figure lurking in the shadow.

When I scrambled though the hole and staggered to my feet, Robin appeared in front of me.

'What have you done?' he yelled.

'Er … ' I wasn't sure I could make sense. 'I couldn't – '

'You couldn't what?'

My head felt heavy and my brain wasn't up to much.

'I couldn't go through with it.'

Robin was not just angry. He was furious.

'Maximum impact. That's what we'd planned. And you've ruined it!'

'I said I didn't want to hurt anybody … '

He grabbed me by the shoulders. 'You fool! I told Beth one of us should – But she wanted someone else to take the blame. Someone who didn't matter.'

'What? But I – ' I couldn't speak any more.

'Why else would she have got you to do it?' Robin sneered at me for what seemed an age. Then he said, 'You'll pay for messing up.' He drew back his arm, ready to thump me with all his strength.

I was drained. An easy target. I began to fall even before his fist landed on my battered face.

It's all a bit of a blur now, but I guess he was off balance on that sloping verge. I guess he wasn't expecting me to crash into him. Maybe, in some desperate attempt at self-defence, I gave him a shove. I'm not sure. Anyway, we both collapsed. I grabbed hold of the bottom of the fence and stuck fast, but he tumbled down the bank. All arms and legs, he toppled towards the road.

I wonder if Robin heard the siren as a fire engine came into view and sped towards the scene of the blast. I wonder if he was dazzled by the headlamps and flashing lights. Out of control, he rolled on to the tarmac. The last thing I remember was the sound of screeching tyres and a stomach-churning thud.

I'd stopped the fireball. I'd saved myself from Robin's fury. But I hadn't saved the planet and I'd done nothing to save Robin. The failed protest had claimed his life.

And that was the end of the Cooler, as

well. I don't mean I changed my views. Sprawled out on the verge, I realised I'd crossed a red line. On one side of it, people didn't get hurt. On the other side, they did. On one side of it, you're a protester. On the other, a terrorist. The tricky part is knowing where to draw the line.

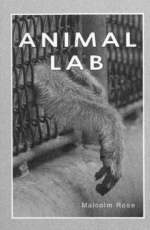

Animal Lab

by Malcolm Rose

Jamie Littlewood is as bald as the monkey he's looking after at the local animal lab. He is happy that the monkey may be the key to curing his baldness. But Jamie's animal rights activist sister makes him think again about what is happening in the lab. What will Jamie do? Who is in the right?

Shouting at the Stars

by David Belbin

For singer Layla it's all a dream come true. Her first album hits the big time and her concerts are all sold out. But a heckler starts to show up at gig after gig and quickly turns everything into a nightmare. Is this just the price of fame for Layla?

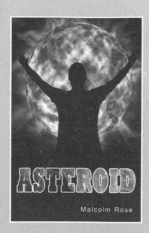

Asteroid

by Malcolm Rose

What can one group of friends do when all of humanity faces extinction? An asteroid is hurtling towards Earth and it will destroy everything on the planet. Josh, Dave and Zack are determined to save planet Earth and the human race. The trouble is, it's impossible – isn't it?

Fighting Back

by Helen Orme

Amita and her family relocate to a new town after her father's business is destroyed in a fire. Hoping for a better life in her new home, Amita is sad when her bitter father refuses to allow her to mix with her white neighbours. She becomes the victim of racial abuse at school. Will she always be hated for being different?

Danger Money

by Mary Chapman

As a World War One recruit onboard the fishing boat the Admiral, all Bob Thompson can think about is how much he will earn. Bob gets danger money, as the ship defends itself against German subs. But by the time Bob realises what he has taken on, it's too late to go back.

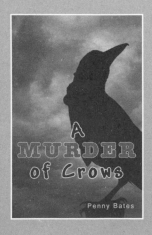

A Murder of Crows

by Penny Bates

Only-child Ben moves to the country with his mum and befriends a crow for company. When a local boy sees this and jeers at him mercilessly, Ben very soon becomes a laughing stock. The bullies want him to hurt the thing he loves the most. But none of them have reckoned on the power of Crow Law!

Doing the Double

by Alan Durant

Twins Dale and Joe are the sons of fallen football ace Nicky Green. They have always joked about swapping their identities for a day, but that was a joke. Now Dale wants Joe to do the double and take his place on the football pitch – for real. How can Joe refuse his twin?

Coming in to Land

by Dennis Hamley

Jack is one of the young cadets chosen by the RAF to learn to fly gliders. The good pilots will go on to fly real planes in the war. But Jack has a fear of coming in to land. Star pupil Cecil thinks Jack shouldn't be flying – and when Jack makes a dangerous mistake, Cecil's determined he'll pay for it.

Invasion

by Mary Chapman

Jack is in hospital – there's something wrong with his leg. But when he catches a glimpse of his X-ray, he doesn't expect to see a huge, squirming thing writhing around inside. It turns out two of his best mates have the same problem. The doctors won't tell them anything. Then the burning and hissing starts.

The Messenger

by John Townsend

When Chris sees a Christmas glass angel smash at his feet, he thinks nothing of it. But then a trip to the moors with his girlfriend brings strange events. They even seem to be moving in time. Was the angel an omen? And what connects past, present and future?